the teacher's mind travels

B.B. Riefner and "Please" at work in Javea, Spain, in 1986

also by B.B. Riefner

A Child Too Near
Satan: A Dog's Story
The Mad, Mad, Magical Misery Tour
Reality Bytes
Mind Travels
The Tarnished Horseman Comes Home,
Slices and Bites from the Pie
I. M. Lawless: The Years of Searching for
Rainbows & Grape Soda

the teacher's mind travels

Stories and Poems by B. B. Riefner

Edited by Alan Abrams

Sligo Creek Publishing Company
Silver Spring, Maryland

Printed in the United States of America

ISBN: 979-8-9911983-1-8

First Edition

Sligo Creek Publishing Company
9039 Sligo Creek Parkway

For my wife, Marilyn, the Dwarf,
who has always inspired and encouraged me
to use continents as stepping stones.

Editor's Note

Six foot plenty, frame of an offensive lineman. Fanatical brows arched above eyes like black holes. Booming voice commanding even the ones sitting in the back row, the ones carving up desktops with their jack knives, the ones who'd jump you in the stairways.

At first you were terrified. And then you were bewildered. Then amused, and finally, when he'd gotten to you, you began to get it.

It was in 1963, things at home were rough, my father's health and career broken by MS. He summoned me from class one morning, walked me out into the hall with his heavy arm around my shoulder. The tweed jacket was scratchy, and his breath powerful with tobacco and coffee. We stopped by the atrium.

Abrams, he barked. *What's the difference between innocence and ignorance?*

I mumbled some sort of platitude, and then he gave me some advice.

I can't recall a word of that advice. The arm around my shoulder was enough. Regardless, the answer to his question lies somewhere in these pages.

Contents

Introduction

Student Tim R's First Day Impressions

Big like tree, dark like night
Eyes of coal
Covered, by textured fur
That radiates its
Insular, northern natures …
Ferocity in look
Braided with a subtle sadness;
Also awed
Of mankind's circumstances.
Compassion …
The knife edge that finds and points,
That divides
The chafe so evenly.
Big bear paws
Which hold the fist,
But could also hold
The breasts of Time
So easily
She would gladly feed us.

Circus Song

Time is a circus, always packing up and moving away.
~Ben Hecht

Part One: Dawn Arrival

Grand Daddy told my Father
one circus tale
each Friday night,
all through the empty winter
just before Daddy went to bed.
He said, "Afterwards, I prayed
in the cold dark
for the Spring magic
parading down Main Street
with the early flowers."
A flow of hopes
from a river of dreams
bringing all
of another's childhood
to sweetly drown him.

***

He claimed the circus snuck into town.
Not even the dogs heard them.
By dawn the cook tent was up
Bread warming and filling
early hopes and smoldering dreams.
That he had fallen in love with love,
peeking under canvas walls,
catching performers behind curtains
of coffee steam. Noticing that
flyers and wirewalkers always touched,
but the star warmed herself by
pressing her cheek into the young clown's shoulder.

***

Grand Daddy claimed,
"All balloon men
carried a legend.
Each balloon
that got away
went right
to a kid
who would never see
a circus.
And that's why
so many balloons
float away."

***

He told Daddy that
the Midway, like magic plants,
grew right up through the sawdust.
And the sideshow tents and rides
popped and bloomed
like giant cornflowers and dandelions.
While tigers and lions and bears
were transformed from
clumps of shrubs and evergreens.

***

That in the smaller circuses
everyone was a clown.
The barker, the blacksmith,
the cook and riggers ...
the chief canvas man,
all melting like butter
on Daddy's pancakes
into clown's masks
three shows a day.

Intermission ... Granddaddy's dead

Part Two: View from the High Wire

Daddy claimed
the tube connecting
the fantasy
the crowd demands
with their necessities of life
is Clown Alley.
And through its colorful funnel
flows the energy
from which all dreams come.

***

He laughed about the circus band
claiming it blew its music out,
but with every breath
it took a gifted kid musician
and sucked him away
from every town they played.

***

He said, "Every circus has a story
about a lion tamer
being knocked out cold
by a tiger.
It's always the poor tiger, son.
And while the assistant
dragged the tamer out,
a clown kept
fifteen cats at bay with just a chair
and a painted grin."

***

And it was Daddy who claimed,
"Freak Alley
calls only to those
whose Karma has been defined
and to those who seek
their hidden ordinations.

To the Boardwalk of Futures
customers go
to walk its length,
choose a costume,
select a booth, and from on high
watch the show
as the Freaks romp by.
Both he and I
one secure...
the other eager...
sought out the Freaks.
One went expecting a preview;
the other to find his friends."

***

Both Daddy and Grand Daddy were sure
since the circus and time began
the stands have overflowed.
Each generation pays gladly
for its special forgetfulness.
And what has been forgotten
still rages through the streets.
But inside the Big Tent the wire walker
never falls.

***

My Daddy always claimed
by making magic an entertainer
blots out changes the world goes through.
"Son, if the magic is great
it erects a dome where life and death
aren't able to penetrate.
And each priest
brings his own illusions,
as reality changes
with every act.
In between
the clowns make the audience
grin at mirrors
less intricate
more clear."
Daddy always claimed

"Life becomes the game.
If there are no artifacts,
there is no magic.
Magic leaves only mystery
through this communion
and clowns sanctify our amusement
which solidifies our faith.
The artist needs the audience.
Their magic needs applause."
Intermission ... Daddy's Dead.

**Part Three: Sifting Daddy's and
Grand Daddy's Memories**

In my dreams I steal a caravan.
A horse drawn circus train
in gaudy array.
Gum dropped colored clowns
clinging like flocks,
overpowering the green and yellow carts,
pulled by pairs of horses
who are Unicorns.
Their red plumes
beckon like temptress' fingers.
Yet, always beyond the children's' reach ...
children of All Ages.
All these promises of Oz,
all this magic,
marches triumphantly up
ramps into the steel drums
of my experiences,
until the lids clang shut
and its immortality is gone.
But not from the magician's wand.

***

Grand Daddy! Some when the circus forgot!
Tradition must remain tradition fills the gaps
between old acts and new faces.
Tradition does not fade
like weathered posters.
But they can be swallowed
by silver tubes
on the minute-less mile
as they roll into town
at 5A.M. unannounced.
And also ... unapplauded.
From below saints and sinners,
cynics and fanatics vow
to pledge themselves anew.

Then rush off into the cold,
through deserts and wildernesses
seeking messages from sands and stars.
While along with a thousand other lunatics
I chase God across stained-glass.
Until God shakes a brush

causing pieces of yesterdays to fall
forming patterns greater than love
always just beyond everyone's reach.

***

Through the telescope of time
which Grand Daddy and Daddy handed me,
the circus celebration blurs.
Vacant lots become dumps
instead of Midways.
Trucks and gas fumes
require no parade permits.
It's not fun to watch
your fantasies and hopes
disappear through armory doors.
The circus cannot understand
doesn't do it alone.
When the admission price ain't high enough
crowds become mobs
with no respect or tolerance
for traditions and customs.
They always demand
only the slick and grand!
Oh, Grand Daddy and Daddy
give me back the Midway!
One that's a century long
leading only to a Big Top
of dreams.
Patched over dreams
which can still
transform vacant lots
into forever Wonderlands!

Give Us This Day Our Daily Dred
or
The Eleven Apostles
or
Glimmering Evils?

Evil is whatever is distracting.
~Franz Kafka

Gods, Goddesses, and Sorcerers

When the sorcerers four appear
Down goes the universe!
Merging magic and madness,
Blending into electronic miracles
As birth bubbles from their fingers
Twilight gods linger upon the fringes
Of their bright promises
That dangle thick as galaxies,
Thin as nebulas, and
Dark, wine blood dregs
Their voices come clearly
Along starlight networks,
And you who listen,
And who trust the endlessness
Of your lives to us,
You may have the energy
But not the magic-
You may hold the light
But not the sun-
You may have the beginning
But never the source-
You may have the instant
But never the motive
And! Because of this,
Down goes the universe.

Questions for Jackson Pollock

If Cane slew Abel and took unto him a wife
And moved East of Eden, did he marry his sister?
If God can make a rock he cannot pick up
Does that still prove God can do anything?
And if gods are merely echoes of our fears and needs,
Is prayer conversing with one's self?
And if so, can we grant wishes, but ignore needs?
And if so, would we lose our minds,
If we could use just twenty-percent of our brains?
If all of mankind's history can be fitted upon a single die
Is it because after a thousand years of mistakes and errors,
We just keep adding … perhaps … etcetera … so on and so
forth?

And if so, how often do mistakes become art?
And if so, does love have to be blind?
So it can survive in this sea of selfishness?
And if so, if beauty is only skin deep,
Why does ugly always go clean through?
And finally…

Does the artist create for his demon?
Or because his demon demands he do so?

An Evening at the Holocaust ...
Or Hollow Cost Museum

The visitors move along the ramps and corridors
As trusting as their ancestors ... as isolated by ignorance or
apathies.

Through narrow passageways, a thousand photogenic faces
Lean down ... their muted screams and cries swept away by
time
Or erased by I-Phones or Reese's
I have viewed those bins stuffed with glass eyes
Artificial limbs akimbo ... shoes sorted by sex
Explored them, super-imposed on my relatives' photographs,
At attention, in their S.S. uniforms, as they peer at
Bunning synagogues packed with sub-human trash
There are no lies or exaggerations ... no sound tracks
Yet there is background music ... whimpers, pleadings and
prayers

A dog barking, a train whistle, and of course
The machine-gun clock announcing another score of bodies
Falling through space and history, into unmarked, neglected
graves

And so, I ask
One day will all happen again?
This time will the Hollow-Cost
Be in Christ's name ... again?

A Hint of Hope

Stealing flowers
From the Mount of the Beatitudes
Reminds the Pilgrim to ask,
How much of God has been stolen …
From afar,
Wrapped in Good Friday's mist,
The Horns of Hitten scream
How can you steal God?
With just a thumb
And Forefinger
The Pilgrim smiles.

Lord of the Manor

From the forest fringed in autumn,
Across the meadows
Ankle deep
In children's dreams,
Over the merry brook
Echoing familiar nursery rhymes,
And through the blooming roses
Guarding the memories
Of my narrow, unclogged,
Boyhood lanes ...
In my village square
The cathedral squats ...
Club in hand,
Snarling and demanding
More thoughts to crush!

Lost Among the Apps

Adolescents of all ages
Come and go
Ignoring more than Michelangelo,
Eyes glued to ill-shaped phones,
Which reduce life, love or death
To less than my hand's size
And as their world expands
Its dimensions do not
Yet, no one dares to yell
"Beware! Take care!
God isn't the only demon
In there!"

The Rejected Request

Come! Just for the brief,
Less than three-billionths
Of your life's span
Embrace the wonders
You refuse to admit
Are poised just beyond
The confines of that box
Your prejudices have
Forced you to erect
Its forces present
Not terror ...not fear
Just change!

Climb, Climb Down Sunset Mountain

If I were more the historian
I would say,
"There will come a time
When we all awake
And begin our journey to Golgotha.
That when we arrive
We have to landscape our own hill,
Search out timbers, tools and nails.
Construct our crosses,
And then,
Become our executioner.
Once we are nailed up,
Our sides punctured
And died ... We awake
And no Marys!
And no end to this!

Birthing Instructions

When I'm dead,
Get someone to chainsaw me up
Then shove me into an old, oil drum.
And when that's done,
Ask all my enemies to come …
Everyone should have
A crowd at their last rites
Hold mine up behind the abandoned shopping center
At night, when only junkies gather,
And where the footing is slippery from grease
A place where only Jacobs sleep
In abandoned telephone booths
Then lay out a feast
Of all the junk food I would not eat.
Let everyone beat on the drum
Ask them all, to be a pal
And piss on it, when it's cherry red
Let them speak the truth about my life …
The one they collided with
But remind them all that their tomorrows
Will always be worse than my yesterdays
Tell them that back then
My sky once held stars at night
And they could see watery reflections.
And how the sun came up clear and hot
Just like my coffin has become …
And have them all sing a song,
Something not too long, and not too new

But please let everyone sing it in tune,
And tell them when they're through
It didn't sound bad at all

But most of all … Before the oil drum
Grows rusty cold again
Remind them all, I promised God
No eye would ever be wet.

When Are You Finally Dead?

Not when you stop breathing,
Not when you stop seeing,
Not when your heart stops …
You are finally dead when
The great expanding,
Magical white light appears.
Accompanied by gales of laughter
And for less than an instant
You wonder who is laughing,
As you speculate if your guess
Was right or wrong?
Then you realize
It is you who is laughing!
Why?
Because suddenly you
Are certain … at this instant …
It doesn't matter.
Which way you guessed.

Rituals

In far away mountains
Los Indians dance
To prevent their world
From reversing direction
In the Plaza Mayor
Old women,
In comfortable shoes
March in circles
To force it.
Los Madres
Carry what remains
Of their murdered children
On cardboard pieces
Or in clear plastic bags.
While the modern world
Hurries by
With cell phones in hand
And a fixed very indifferent stare.

What Your Minister Would Never Tell You ... Etc.

Listen carefully!
If you spend a single Sunday, Friday or Saturday
In a church ... mosque ... synagogue ... etc ...
After your first period,
After your first ejaculation,
All the gods we claim are only one,
Who listen to only your sect demands
Will sit on your face ...
Forever ruining every fuck
For the rest of your life!

And that's
The best
Part of it!

The Eventual Questions ... and Answer

Mary ... Mary ... Virgin Mary
How did the myth of Jesus grow?

"Free fish and bread
And not denying
He could raise dead

And oh yes,
The Mary,
We didn't get to know."

Angel Moments

I think we all have empathy. We may not
have the courage to display it.
~Maya Angelou

The First Moment: Danny Hoffer's Tale

Gordon Angel saved my life. Not in the literally sense but … well, let me finally get this off my chest … or better … my conscience.

Dr. Angel was my Junior-Senior High School Principal. I don't know much about his background except he really had the welfare of his students welded to his six-feet-four-inch, Greek-god-like body. And if it hadn't been for Dr. Angel's role in my life, I would never have become the principal of the largest high school in Parker County.

Actually, another name who had a role in this has to be inscribed in saving my life … but he only opened the door. I don't think Mr. Dean Barber could have taken me any further than he did. So, let's begin with Mr. Barber.

School had been an endless nightmare for me since third grade. Mrs. Frazer, my second-grade teacher, who couldn't teach a fish how to swim, placed me in Special Education for the next year, because she claimed I had real problems reading and doing math. That was slightly true when it came to word problems in math, but I could read okay … I guess.

The second day in my ninth grade Special Ed. Class Mr. Barber walked by the open back door, saw me sitting against the wall and stopped long enough to give me a wave. Ten minutes later I was out of Mrs. Trent's nightmare and seated in the first row of Mr. Barber's U.S. History class. I loved any kind of history, so I didn't dare ask him why I was there. However, he was on my case as soon as I showed up for Flag Football practice. I was his hands-down choice for quarterback as soon as he saw me throw a pass about forty yards with a perfect spiral.

"Why were you in Special Ed, Danny?" he asked after practice. As soon as he saw it was going to take more than ten seconds he told me he wanted to see me after practice and he'd drive me home. This was almost forty years ago. Maybe we should make that four worlds ago? Now-a-days he'd be fired on the spot, but back then teachers kept kids in detention and actually did drive them home.

After I explained he wanted to know if I thought I was dumb, how come I had my hand up to answer every question he asked about the causes of the Civil War? And I told him I had read a lot about it and I loved history.

That was in his office but on the ride to my home he asked if I had been diagnosed with reading problems, did someone read it for me ... I said, sometimes they did ... but just a little ... Only when the words were too multisyllabic. That I had good listening ears and remembered everything I ever heard.

I got out in front of the apartments. I didn't want him to know Momand I were living in a small storage room next to the boiler room. That was illegal, but we paid off our janitor. Or there was only one spigot running cold water and we used a camp stove to cook on. I took a shower at school, and thanked God I had gym every day, so I could do that.

I also didn't want him to know that Mom was a chronic drunk, spent all the money she made cleaning offices on ninety-eight cent wine. So, I had to get up at four, seven days a week to serve two paper routes and run errands after school for the local food market and hide my earnings, so we could pay the rent and get something to eat!

It really got dicey for me when Mr. Barber told me I should run for president of the ninth grade. That was after we had won four of our first five games and I was sort of a hero when I tossed two touchdown passes late in the last two games to win them.

I resisted ... for maybe a day. Well, until Mr. Barber just put my name in and made me give a speech in front of the whole school! I nearly crapped in my pants when he told me! It was insane!

He helped me make up a speech with a lot of jokes mixed up in what I wanted my class to accomplish during the school year and I won ... hands down!

Things were going okay until Mom found out where I hid the money and stole some for her boozing. So, I had to start carrying it with me. When she discovered that, she yelled at me for an hour … at least. But I refused to give her any, so she called the cops and had me arrested, claiming I had physically assaulted her. She even had a couple of recent bruises and a self-inflected scratch as evidence.

I got the right to one phone call. I didn't know Mr. Barber's number but I did know Laura Dustin's. She was my VP. I had to tell her I was in Juvenile Detention, because there was no way he could contact me other than coming to me. Laura promised she wouldn't tell a soul. She never did …and oh yeah … we've been married for thirty- one years.

Couple hours later a matron took me into the conference room and there was Mr. Barber and Dr. Angel! It blew my mind so badly I started crying!

Dr. Angel made me tell him everything from soup to nuts. He never showed the least sign that what I said was concerning him. But when I finished he told me to stay there and he'd be back. About an hour later he came in and told me we could go! We went right by the front desk, and the officer waved at us as we did.

Dr. Angel drove a Caddy sedan with all the trimmings. I wasn't sure what was going down, so I stayed mute. About half an hour later we pulled up in front of a nice-looking house and he told me to come with him. Turned out the house belonged to Mrs. Geiger, who was one of our Guidance counselors. She was at the front door before he rang the bell.

It turned out I stayed with her for a couple days, and then Dr. Angel sent for me after school ended. He told me I was going to meet three groups of people who were thinking about becoming my legal guardians! That I was to act natural and see how things went … Oh … he added if I liked a particular set to wink.

I winked at each one of them. The Anderson family decided I would be a perfect fit. They had two other adopted boys who were younger than I was and they thought I could be a good influence. I was.

So, let's get to the end of this … okay? That was the last time I ever saw Mom. I played football in high school. Got a scholarship and sort of played some in college. Dr. Angel and Mr. Barber came to any home game. I majored in International Economics and graduated with honors. However, after five years with Ford Motor Credit I couldn't understand how I could be unhappy when I was streaking up the ladder toward a really well-paying position. Then, I realized I was guilt ridden. That I should be paying back for my good fortune.

I went back to Dr. Angel and after I explained my mindset he made a couple of phone calls and two weeks later I was hired by Carter County as a Social Studies teacher. I married, had a son and daughter who were very successful, but not as educators. Twelve years later, Lara and I went to Dr. Angel's funeral last month ... I had the honor of doing the eulogy, and never mentioned what he did for me. There were too many other important events. But I do admit I cried a lot after I got off the podium. Didn't want to let go in front of at least three hundred people. We had standing room only.

The Second Moment: J. D. Salinger and Me

Before we get into this, let me make one simple statement: All a school system needs to be successful is a superintendent who gets enough money to support it, and devoted principals determined to select good teachers. The usual supervision positions are created to get those who cannot or will not teach out of the classroom.

So, Benjamin Harrison's faculty is having its first meeting for its third school year and no one is expecting Dr. Angel to open with the following.

"It is obvious that we didn't do our job last year. My phone didn't ring half as many times as it did our first. If I'm not defending you from irate parents for the content you are teaching or the method you are using, we are not fulfilling our academic obligations."

Before we even had a chance to defend ourselves Angel added ...

"I just got the results for our Iowa Tests for Educational Standards. On a scale where fifty percent indicates a student may successfully attend college and over seventy-five percent guarantees success if the student is so inclined, what do you think was the average score for our entire student body? Any offerings ... None? ... Well how about our lowest students received a seventy-eight percent rating?"

He went on to tell us he had never seen anything like this and that our kids demanded we exert ourselves to maximum intellectual efforts. To explore and question ... to allow far ranging topics to the max and he finished with:

"We have got to get back to reaching out and offering them an academic smorgasbord."

When a fairly large group of Jewish parents asked me not to teach the Holocaust, because it was never going to happen again, I assured them that it would if we buried it. One of the fathers said he would have to speak to Angel to prevent this ... even though they all claimed I was an excellent teacher and they loved their kids arguing over points in my homework ... almost all the others nodded. So, until he made his declaration, most of last year I wondered why Angel hadn't asked to see me.

It only took two days into the year for me to show up at his office door. When I asked him just why in the hell he was giving me the brightest bunch of ninth grade imps who were always raising the bar no matter what, he motioned for me to take a seat.

"Arthur, you're getting the top two ninth grade groups, because I do not want Sam Fredrick anywhere near them. I can't get rid of him, so he is getting the bottom tier ... and even then ... anyway is that why you came in?"

I nodded and then he added that when kids asked hard to answer questions good teachers, like most of our faculty, said, "Let's look into that. It really sounds interesting."

He stunned me a bit when he said he liked my idea of letting both groups try to build a new world while I showed them all the flaws we had made to date. I wanted to know how he knew that. Had parents called? And he told me no. When I insisted, he said he stood in the hall after school looking to see that they were carrying books home. He claimed he also asked them what was going on in specific classrooms.

So, I went back to the intellectual jungle ... maybe circus is better ... where I had to confront twenty-six or so vicious lions and tigers and bears four hours a day, twice a day without a whip, or gun, even a chair ... and I loved it.

We were half-into the second grading period when I read J.D. Salinger's "A Perfect Day for Banana Fish" aloud, because both sections had just finished, Leo Tolstoy's _Anna Karenina_ and were fixated on Leven having a mystical revelation while working in the fields with the peasants. The connection was the kids had to understand the challenges they had to face once they started over _Fool's Hill._ That is the time when they had difficulty ignoring their urges to do irrational things. Research says that's about twenty-four. That explains a lot ... right?

Nature called just over half-way through my second class. I knew they could be trusted to carry on their discussion and a bathroom was only a classroom away. My Angel Moment began the instant I started in through the open back door and saw our Senior High Social Studies Supervisor, Miss Holly Safford, sitting at my desk. I don't know why I decided to stay out of view … at least to her … and go stand just outside my front door.

Joy Danner led the discussion about how desperate Leven became when he could not convey his revelation. She noticed me but made no effort to acknowledge my presence. The period was about to end and they concluded there could be nothing worse than having this experience and not be able to convince others you had had it.

That's when Felix Greenberg, the top cognitive scorer and most artistically talented in the room said there was something a lot worse. Just then he was standing on a step ladder doing a black and white rendition of Mantegna's "Caesar's Funeral Possession" which took up the entire bulletin-board running the length of my room.

Joy glared and said he always had something that topped whatever they were doing so what could be worse? Felix added a final touch to the chariot and descended before dropping his bomb.

"Not being able to forget that you had it, Joy. That's the worst ain't it?"

And the dismissal bell ended that … for now. But it opened the door for my Moment when I stepped in and Holly rose, cocked her swagger stick under her left arm like a member of the Royal House Guards and said, "I'll see you in Dr. Angel's office. This is your planning period, correct?

I deliberately got ahead of her as we went forth to whatever.

The Boss was seated behind his desk and two straight-backed chairs faced him.

Holly leaned menacingly as she grimly narrated that after I read "Banana Fish" aloud many of my kids bought the paperback edition and read all *Nine Stories*.

"Dr. Angel, I don't think you have read any of this insignificant author, so you wouldn't know that there is also a very salacious story, 'Pretty Mouth and Green My Eyes' also in that edition."

"Holly, did you discover this because a parent or parents called you?"

"No, but they could have and I haven't been informed yet. Several of your staff gave me that information."

Instantly, I knew it was Sam, Harriet Bing and Ida Anderson, the other ninth grade Core teachers. It amazed me he didn't pursue this.

"Well, Holly you're inferring that if our kids read Bret Harte's 'Outcasts of Poker Flat,' from our ninth grade English text, some of them might like it and buy one of his other books with salacious stories. Then, our county would have to discard twenty thousand texts … right?"

Holly's expressions indicated fury, frustration, and fear.

"That seems a bit too farfetched, Dr. Angel."

"Hardly. However, that really isn't what I wish to convey."

The Boss rose and moved to the picture window looking out into our stunningly pupil inspired, landscaped courtyard.

"Holly, ever since I had to tolerate your incompetence at Bruce High, I've been looking for a valid excuse to tell you, I will no longer allow you to observe as long as I am principal here. Thank you and that will be all."

"Oh yes, Mr. Carter, please remain while I escort Mrs. Safford to her car."

Holly stormed out, denying The Boss his moment of glory. He didn't give me any breathing room either.

"If you got a copy here, get it to me by the end of the day. And Carter don't get the idea you have any personal gain regarding this. I'm going to read that story and the other one and I'll get back to you."

So happened, a well worn Salinger was resting in my desk. Next morning there was a note from the Boss to see him immediately. Every part of me that was suspended tightened as I complied.

As I entered, I caught J.D. as it came floating over his desk.

"Sit down. No … this won't take long."

Now other parts of me squished. I wondered if I could get a job before the bank fore-closed on my loan.

"Like most people who are uninspired, and disinterested in life's problems, Holly has really gotten bad reviews on Mr. Salinger. I was up over half the night reading all nine of his stories and Art, he is a major, major writer. Oh yeah, I also see why you read 'The Banana Fish.' Now, get out of here.

And don't bust your inflated, ego expanded head on the doorsill."

My inhaled breath exploded and The Boss laughed, waved my dismissal and sent me back to the reality of Felix Greenburg's offerings.

The Third Moment: Uniform Isn't Always Uniformed

This goes back years … worlds actually. Attending Gordon Angel's funeral was like having a ninety-six inch TV projecting over a segment of it.

Oh, sorry, I'm Sandra Cohen; 1963 Ben Harrison Grad. Let me begin this by saying, I had to have a lot of guts to ask to see Dr. Angel when I was only a tenth grader. However, I thought the circumstances warranted me telling him what Darin Silverberg had concocted for our World History class the next day.

Darin was about five inches above five feet and he wasn't going to get any taller. Therefore, he was full of insane crap that drove most of our crew out the doors. I mean they loved his creativity! However, what he got all but me to agree to do in Mr. Sam Fredrick's class could have gotten us all suspended … maybe expelled.

Darin really resented Mr. Fredrick handing out mimeographed sheets with the basic outline system already printed. He claimed Fredrick was treating us like we were fourth or fifth-graders. Actually, that was when we learned how to do outlining. And once we got to junior high all of our teachers were surprised and pleased to find that out.

Fredrick's page had Roman Numerals for Main Topics, capitals for most important events or names. And on and on, right down to small letters in parentheses. After three days of that, Darin said we should all dress like we were elementary kids, and Janet Frazer said maybe like Catholic school kids. Since we Jewish kids dominated 10-C, I thought that was adding insult to injury.

Darin wanted all the girls in white blouses and black skirts, no makeup and hair pulled back in ponytails. Janet said the guys should be in black slacks and white, button-down shirts with formal ties. And also, we were all to have ballpoint pens that clicked like loading a bullet into a rifle's chamber. By the end of the next period when I discovered I was the only hold out, I decided I had to tell Dr. Angel.

I was amazed when he sort of smiled as I got to the end and the pens. He thanked me and gave me a hall pass. I thought that was the end of it … ha!

Since I was out of uniform ... sorry, Darin made me sit in the last seat right by the door. From there I watched Dr. Angel leaning against the door sill as the class went through its gyrations, and smiling as long as he was there. That was about ten minutes.

Then, next day I was about to enter Mr. Harvey's science lab when I heard Mr. Carter laughing. He was relating yesterday's antics and I didn't interrupt him. I wanted to hear if Dr. Angel had had any reactions beyond what I had seen. The words are engraved in my cerebral cortex for the rest of my life.

The Boss is in the lounge when Fredrick comes in with Wilson and Harper and he didn't see Angel. He's ... like on cloud nine. Tells them wait until they see how well 10-C is dressed and how they took his instructions. He claimed it was the very first time they had obeyed without question when he handed out the outline sheets and did exactly as they were told the entire period. By then, Harvey is breaking up a little. But then he said he was gonna laugh when he realized Fredrick hadn't a clue.

Also, he wanted to laugh so hard he ran in the bathroom, and Dr. Angel was about one step behind him. Even so, they both had to stuff some toilet paper in their mouths to keep anyone in the room from hearing them laughing.

When I told Darin, he almost crapped in his pants. And he swore he was ready to do it again. Well, after two weeks I asked him when, because now I really wanted to join. But he said Dr. Angel called him in that day and told him he would be suspended if he did that again. But much later he told me Dr. Angel had laughed and made him promise he would behave. That never was any part of Darin's behavior even to this day ... and I thank God it isn't.

The Fourth Moment: The Grub Stake and Me

Whoever expects a guy to get out of a stretch limo, come in your back door's classroom with a case of twenty-five year old Veuve-Cliequot, Demi-Sec Champagne. I never learned how to pronounce it ... our French teacher was on maternity leave. I do know it costs two-hundred- and fifty dollars a bottle. He was also saying it was mine, but also wondering aloud why Mr.

Leonard had just rejected a ten thousand dollar check as a reward for teaching him how to do some intricate cut on a wood lathe?

Okay ... this actually happened about three hours ago ... Half-way through my so-called planning period. His name is Timothy Grubb. Maybe I should give a little background before we get into what just occurred. Oh ... I kept the dozen bottles. Have never had a glass that good till now.

Timothy entered my Eleventh Grade Advanced Placement Modern U.S History class three weeks into May. I checked his grades from a school in Akron, Ohio. They were mostly B's except he aced Art and Industrial Arts, at Benjamin Harris is in Maryland. Last year we dropped the Junior High part. Right then we had a staff of one hundred and nineteen teachers and an eighteen hundred plus student body.

After a couple days, Tim seemed to fit right into Ben's flow. He never raised his hand to answer a question but gave thought provoking answers when I called on him. A fellow student, Georgia Forman, a 9.5 on a scale of 10 for good looks, took him under her wing ... for want of a better body part.

School had just ended, and I had gone into Dan Fuller's wood shop to finish a lamp. He was staring out one of his eight windows, Dan was so intensely focused on what was going on in the back parking lot I had to nudge him to get his attention.

When I saw the mob of kids sort of forming a circle and Tim squared off against Bernard Kingsley the school bully, I started for the door to stop it.

Dan stayed me, saying maybe if we give this kid a chance he might just beat the snot out of Kinsley. That didn't seem possible until he told me to size things up. Tim seemed to be attached to Kinsley's torso, delivering short jabs that traveled no more than six or eight inches. Once I saw Bernie's face bouncing back and forth, I held back. And Tim not only beat the snot out of the bastard, he also took off his bloodied sweatshirt and gave it to Bernie. Later, I found out he made him take it home and wash it.

Just then, Dr. Angel came round the corner, and everybody but Tim and Bernie fled. They stayed, because Tim was holding his adversary by his neck. The Boss escorted the pair inside and suspended Kingsley for a school week on the spot. I was surprised when he drove Tim home.

Next day in the teacher's lounge my closest confident, Georgia Kolb, told me Grubb had jumped up from his desk in her room and raced into Harriet Hawks, across the hall and prevented Kingsley from physically assaulting her. That led to the after-school conflict. Harriet had informed Angel as soon as school ended, and that was why The Boss hadn't suspended Tim.

That Friday after school I joined Dr. Angel and two other guys for a round of golf. We were discussing Tim before we teed up for the second hole.

Angel said the kid had spent his entire summer vacation at a Juvenile Detention Center in Akron for physically assaulting a mature male. Claimed Tim's record stated he could have been charged as an adult, but there were extenuating circumstances ... i.e. ... he might have been defending a paraplegic veteran who was confined to a wheelchair. The verdict of summer confinement resulted when the vet didn't show for the trial.

Tuesday night was darts at the pool pallor. Our team was leading the league, but that didn't keep me from asking why Tim was hunched over the first table in a five- and ten-dollar nine ball game. Fred, the owner told me Tim worked Saturdays sweeping and re-racking. But he was also a really budding pool shark.

The following Monday when Kingsley came back from suspension, The Boss quietly assigned Tim as Ms. Hawks teacher's aide for the term's last three weeks. Naturally peace prevailed.

None of us knew he also hired Tim to do lawn maintenance at his home. Or that he tutored him in math, so he could take Calculus his senior year. Or he arranged for a childless family to become his foster parents. Seems Tim's stepfather liked to beat on him ... that is until Tim decided to fight back. Then, the stepdad began abusing his mother and ... well ... The Boss kept that from coming to trial, also. That all came out at Dr. Angel's farewell dinner two years after Tim graduated and joined the Marines. Tim told all, wearing his full-dress blues with three combat ribbons after the ceremony, and a couple of beers.

Anyway, before he could leave, I asked Grubb what went with trying to give Mr. Fuller ten grand. He sat on the edge of my desk, asked if he could smoke and I nodded. I wanted to know what was what.

Tim said Dan had taught him how to do the taper cut, and after the Marines he wanted to become either a pool shark or start a business making cue sticks. In a couple months he found out he was good, but not good enough for the former and not skilled enough for the latter. That's when he came back and Dan showed him how one Saturday morning.

Said it was an immediate success and when he sold it to AMC for almost two million and he had almost 16,000 orders. At a hundred and fifty each he had back orders for over a million bucks. So, that was why he wanted to give Dan a reward.

Mr. Fuller told me to buy electronic stuff for the poverty stricken schools in our county. There are plenty of those.

When I asked about the case of wine, he grinned and said I was responsible for him marrying Georgia Forman. Said I had told her to be very careful, but I thought he was a good guy. They just had their second son.

When I confronted The Boss about all he had done and Tim had stopped by, he told me they had been in contact since the day he drove him home after the fight. He said it like ...well, it wasn't a big deal. Like, didn't everybody do that?

The Fifth Moment: Three Black Trash Bags
And Silos Aren't Always for Wheat

This all begins when I open the door to my classroom at 7:30 AM. For a few seconds I do not see the body stretched across my desk. It's face down, facing the smeary windows, so I can't identify who it is. My physical being wants to rush over, but mentally I hold back … if it is really a corpse, I shouldn't touch it. Then it sits up and I let go with, "Kurt Carter! What the hell's … heck's going on?"

He slides off the desk, and almost leaps as he throws both his arms about me.

He's crying. Nope, he's sobbing. Sobbing so hard I hug back, then place him in my chair, and ask him again. His response bounces off all four walls and is etched in my memory till this day.

"Mr. Harmon, yesterday was my sixteenth birthday. I went home wondering if Dad and Mom were gonna let me get my Learner's Driver's License, or tell me we're going out for dinner. There's an envelope stuck to the front door. I thought it was a birthday card. But I couldn't figure out why my key wouldn't open it. Or why there were three really big green trash bags sitting over by the swing. So I sat on it and opened the letter. Here, you read it. If I read it aloud I'll bawl my head off, again ."

I took it, and later was glad I squatted on the desk's edge. I read it silently. I'm not going to tell you all of it … Just the parts that cut right through to my gut.

It said that he was sixteen and they were tired of supporting him and Kurt not returning that, by getting good grades or an after-school job to help out. That said, they had sold the house and were moving to a cheaper place. They had enclosed a check for seventy-five dollars and said that as long as he made no efforts to contact them, they would send the same amount once a month.

(Side Bar: They never did.)

Finally, all his clothes were in the three bags. All of them had been washed, or dry cleaned.

So, I took him to Dr. Angel and the next part of Kurt's life went main stream.

Angel heard him out, told me I could go, and when I checked after lunch he had made arrangements for him to temporarily stay with Mr. Luther, our Auto Mechanic's Instructor. Turned out the temporary part lasted until he had graduated, gone to our state university and entered the United States Air Force as a second lieutenant.

Even though Luther and I did not get along socially, I always thought matching Kurt up with him was really weird. Jonathan Luther was an ex- naval fighter pilot. Every time I confronted him about Kurt he always opened the conversation by asking me how could an ex-Marine end up with a full-faced beard and hair that touched his shoulders? I ignored it after the second time it was offered. But I am certain Luther made Kurt meet his standards from personal hygiene to answering with *Yes sir, no sir or no excuse sir!*

It was my final year when I told a knock on my office door to enter … I was now Principal of Benjamin Harrison High. I decided a week after I got the job I could never fill Angel's shoes … but I tried to live up to his expectations. The imposing figure of a USAF major, in full uniform with a couple rows of ribbons blind-sided me for about five seconds and then I blurted out, "Kurt Naylor!" Jumped up, reaching out to grasp a vise like return.

It took thirty minutes or so after a couple of beers at Bennie's to get the full story.

Kurt's excellent grades and ROTC ratings got him assigned to the Strategic Air Command, based in Nebraska. He spent two years training as a B-52 pilot and was disappointed when he was assigned to a Missile Silo containing four twenty megaton missiles … as he said … *Enough to destroy most of New England and add in lots of New York.*

Then, he told me he had retired and just dropped by to see Mr. Luther and decided he'd come and see me. He said he wasn't surprised that I made Principal. He asked about Angel and I told him he died from natural causes is 1999 at ninety-four. He said that he deserved to live even longer.

That's when I asked him why he was getting out before doing twenty years and getting a good pension? There are times when I wished I hadn't asked.

"It was okay as long as I wasn't commanding. What the hell, twenty-four hours, two hundred feet underground is normal ain't it? Actually, we had three shifts so it's only the normal eight-hour workday. Well, only that as long as we didn't have a drill. Drills called all three shifts to their stations, Dr. Harmon."

I had no idea what was consuming his brain, so I let him decide just how far he wanted to take his confession. That's something else I wish I had been able to step away from … but I didn't.

"Oh, there are four big belly busters that only represented our contribution. We have about fifteen hundred various sizes of atomic missiles … enough to crack the earth's crust and maybe get rid of eighty percent of the population. Some instantly … the unlucky would take maybe a full year.

"So, there you are… all these codes flashing across the Teleprompters … changing engagement levels from low to max. That's when the 'Use Them or Lose Them' takes over. Proceeding to the various stages that are required to arm our missiles, and wondering how many silos … you get it, don't you?"

Of course I didn't. There were some vague mental images of the glaring, gigantic bursts of flames, but I could not grasp his state of mind at that instant, so when I nodded my head Kurt continued.

"Your countdown reaches ten seconds and the code board says Presidential permission has been fully granted. So, maybe this is the instant when you realize all your training has been focused solely on you becoming auto-metastasized. That you have been brainwashed and will command the launch … no questions asked, no regrets and …

"At three seconds the inter-com declares, 'This is a drill … all stations stand down.' You inhale, step back and if this is your initiation you let it all fade into the bleached concrete walls. But after two or three years of it … one drill … one instant between five and three seconds … your brain screams NO MORE and you decide you have to get placed somewhere else. When you are told that is not possible, that your only course is to resign, you obey."

We had one more beer before Kurt said he had to go and he hoped he would get assigned to Ben Harrison High next term. I was surprised when he admitted he wanted to join the ranks. Well, maybe for fifteen minutes. Then, it all made sense. At least the new world he was seeking so desperately, would be one of familiarity or insanity as only a teacher would embrace.

The Sixth Moment:Skip to the Next Level

Even before I began teaching, I was convinced that the Public School Systems were there to provide babysitting service so parents could labor. Later, I discovered that the labor unions wanted kids out of the factories and mines, so they could fight for higher wages and less hours per week. Also, to get better organized and grow.

Sorry … I'm back … Arthur Carter, the guy who has to walk into a cage filled with snarling, blood thirsty teenagers who want to eat my brain. Oh, and see how often they can ask questions which will either embarrass or befuddle me.

This kind of kid is going to learn no matter what. They are the exceptions and believe me most of my fellow educators despise and hate them. The average teacher is determined they will do everything possible to force them into intellectual ping-pong balls. You know, same size, same color and able to bounce only a certain height.

There is also another device the educational system uses. Send the best students to the worst teachers who follow the Golden Rule … which is;

Written on the board is the following daily class assignment.

1.   *Read pages 219-233.*
2.   *Answer the questions on Page 234 and 235.*
3.   *If you complete this before the class ends go to page 236 and answer questions 1-4 for extra credit.*

The teacher sits at their desk pretending to grade papers. They do not tolerate verbal questions. Some are known to sneak Vodka-laced coffee or tea during class time, discreetly of course.

It's the last week of school, when Rita Morningside raps on my door. Rita was in my class two years ago. Straight A's in all her classes. Never volunteered, sat in a front seat, took copious notes and turned in assignments that were so advanced, creatively, and precisely I sought them out and shoved them under the other sixty or so weekly essays. I waved her in. For five or so minutes I asked the routine questions. How were her grades, who were her teachers at Harrison High and what classes were coming up for her senior year?

She spent a couple sentences telling me how much she had enjoyed my class; in fact all of her ninth grade classes. That she had made the National Honor Society at the end of her sophomore year … because she was already taking some senior courses in math and science. And then she dropped all the sham and asked if she could sit down and ask me a very serious question.

I nodded but I wasn't ready for it.

"I don't want to waste time taking my senior year at Harrison. Every one of the senior teachers are… "

"Well county regulations say you can't skip it and go to college. Rita"

She acknowledged that but asked if she could get Dr. Angel to talk to her. I said that would be no trouble and was surprised when he agreed to see her immediately.

Rita explained her predicament and that brought a strange but hasty grin from The Boss.

He went through the same routine as I had but then he added, "But I think there is a way you can side step it Rita. All you need to graduate is Problems of Democracy and English Four, correct?"

Rita nodded and I could see the hopes rising as she did.

"Well, why don't you go over to Fairmount County, and take them there this summer? Morris High must be less than a mile from your home. You can get the two English normal day times and the Social Studies in the evening. Of course you are going to have to pay out of county fees which aren't something to sneeze at."

Rita said her family would have no problems with that. Angel smiled and wished her God Speed and she literally sailed out of his office.

After she was out of hearing range The Boss leaned back and bellowed. Then he swung toward me and let loose.

"Art, every word she said about that Dumb-Down Crew is not only true, it's letting them off lightly. I could go on for hours but just let me tell you one example.

"Mrs. Ruth, the 12th Grade English teacher spends the entire first week rehearsing fire drills. She sends them through all the various ways for exiting the building. Even assigns certain students to lead each evacuation. And I've had five of our kids come and tell me that she says if all of the exits are blocked they will return to their room and the three strongest boys will jump to the ground and then catch each student as they follow. And Art ... she is on the third floor! That's at least twent- five feet of free fall!"

I wasn't back for the Fall Term five minutes when he told me all had gone well and Rita was enrolled at Duke, and sent him a nice letter thanking both of us for our advice. My letter was waiting for me when I dumped my mail on my desk.

Now here's the best part. Rita destroyed the system. The next year over twenty of the best students at Harrison follow her path and broke the entire system. Two years later, the Dumb-Down Crew had either retired or been reassigned to lower stations.

The Boss gloated silently but he did tell me that Dr. Horace Hector, Harrison's Principal, presumed he was the only intelligent principal in the entire world and had handpicked the Dumb-Down Crew because they kowtowed twenty-four hours a day. However, The Boss was disappointed that Hector did not let his raging ego have him seek a position at The Board.

The Seventh Moment: The Alphabet is Not in Order

There must be five other teachers who want to narrate the alphabet fiasco but I, Arthur Carter have not only seniority, but also longest tenured status. Once again it involves one of the *Terrible Threesome ...* Mrs. Donna Wilson, English Department Chairperson.

It's mid-January, 1964 and Dr. Angel has insisted *Team Teaching* is the most effective way to reach the total intellectual spectrum our student body spans. Everyone on the faculty ... this includes the *Terrible Threesome*, admits we are really dealing with caged animals when it comes to the average I.Q. Even the kids in Industrial-Arts were there not because they are in the lower intelligence ranges, but because they are from a different economic bracket. Which is the sixty percent of Americans who detest academics and consider school a brief interruption before they can quit ... climb on the train ... get a good paying factory job ... get married ...buy a house and raise their kids ...who will also hate education.

Just then I had thirty-one ninth graders where the lowest I.Q. was the ninety-second percentile. They had decided they wanted to construct a new world and see if they could correct or avoid all the mistakes and screw ups the present world offered. After I said they might consider letting women run it, they decided I was going to go over all the historical errors beginning with Eve and the Serpent!

We were halfway there and the great revelation they had arrived at was they were forced to accept the very institutions they knew had caused all the problems. Why? Because they came to the realization that it was greed, superstitions and religious concepts that made the world go round.

Two good examples ... theocracy and capitalism were the chosen political and economic systems because the first controlled our behavior from the womb to the tomb; the second was the only one which seemed to foster growth at the present stage of our social development ... economic and social.

Now, I was thrust into a situation where we were into the third week of the experiment and I had yet to see any of my former students. Why? Well, because *The Terrible Threesome* controlled who got when, where and for what. When it comes to competing with me, I am sure that they consider me a pending plague.

So, here's how this all went down.

I'm having lunch with nine angry kids who want to know when I get re-involved in their academic lives and Darin pops in, wearing his usual evil grin. However, it seems to have grown, so I ask him what's up?

Darin winks and says all he is going to tell me is not to miss second period tomorrow when half of the tenth grade will have their first large lecture. He did add, as the bell ending lunch rang and they were off to see whomever, "Mrs. Wilson is presenting."

Once they were gone and I was getting ready to walk the halls, Darin pushed my door open and added, "See if you can get Dr. Angel interested, too."

Well, I ignored that, but next day I was half hidden by the lunchroom's double doors, waiting for the bell to ring. The area was packed with kids. The lunch benches were set in nine rows, and six deep. Then, I felt a hand on my shoulder and heard Dr. Angel say he wanted to see me after this.

The bell rang. Donna stepped out from behind the stage curtains and took her place behind the podium. She placed her notebooks on it and spoke into the microphone.

"Alright … Girls and boys, I want you all sitting on the back side of the benches, so you are facing me."

Before anyone really began rushing for the desired backseats she added, "and I want you in alphabetical order … that's according to your last name."

The sea of wild beasts froze. I did notice that Katherine Zeller nodded and grinned at Bob Abbot. Then, the vocal response flooded the place. I turned to see if *The Boss* was still there and his expression was as startled as mine. But he signaled not to comment, and watch.

The melee must have gone on for at least four or five more minutes before Wilson leaned into the mike and called out. "Alright! Alright! Sit anywhere."

That started the stampede I had expected. "But be sure you are all facing front!" she continued. "And get your …

When I decided to turn, *The Boss* motioned for me to

follow him. I was surprised when he didn't head for his office. Instead we ended up sitting in his Caddy.

I could describe his bewilderment and sullen rage at the stupidity, but you fill in the blanks. He did declare that the next day I would meet with the divided entire tenth grade ... for ninety minutes each time.

When I asked him what he wanted me to do, he said, "What you always do. Entertain them, as you educate, Carter. Go in there and save my program."

I want to save the rest of this for another time. So, let's get to what really blew my mind.

Next morning Alex Harrison is standing in the doorway to my office ... it used to be a book storage room ... and when I nodded, he entered. Alex was twelve and in the tenth grade because his I.Q. is in middle-genius status. He had already taken all our math courses, and is enrolled at the state university for advance courses.

"Mr. Carter, did you know there aren't twenty written alphabets?"

"Alex, what in the world are you telling me?'

"That Mrs. Wilson told us since we didn't know where we were supposed to sit we had to write the alphabet twenty times."

"And of course Mr. Harrison, you are in deep do-do. Go away before you contaminate my office"

An hour later *The Boss* shows up and tells me he had to suspend Alex for three days. But also, that his parents both held sensitive positions at John's Hopkins University, so *The Boss* wanted to arrange an in-school suspension. He asked if Ryan Hardy our advanced math teacher, and Jerry Sloan, Science Department Chairperson, should find something to keep him busy for that time. I nodded. We decided to put him out at the football field and see if he could estimate the number of cubic yards of dirt that had to be removed.

Ryan said, "That'll fix that bright little devil. He's got to know advanced calculus. "

Well, it didn't. Alex showed up right after lunch with an answer, Ryan had to call the university to see if it was valid. It was ... actually, less than an eighth of a meter too much.

They wanted to know who did the work and he told them. Two weeks later Dr. Angel told us the National Observatory had invited Alex to come by any Thursday evening and look through their telescope.

Oh yeah. Harrison had to turn in weekly lesson plans from them until she transferred the end of the term. Sam Fredrick got the same medicine and joined her.

That makes two down … and one to go.

The Eighth Moment: The Green Tattoo

The startled, immaturely pitched male curses and girlish screams pulled me though my open classroom door like I was being sucked into a Black Hole. That mental image vanished the instant I realized I was confronted by a pair of blood splattered, tenth-grade males just dismissed   from my Biology class.

Kurt Naylor was stretched face down on the terrazzo floor. A small but growing blood pool surrounded his head.

Joel Davis stood over him with his forehead covered with blood seeping down over his nose and chin before defacing his button-down shirt.

I yelled what was going on, centering on Joel, who didn't even shrug as he said something about Naylor being way out of line. I was about to order him to the nurse's office and help Naylor to his feet, so he could join Davis.

Then, I realized there weren't any sources for Davis's bleeding. So, I stepped closer until I could see the small bruise slowly spreading across his forehead. That compelled me to reach down and help Naylor up.

The facial damage was extensive. He had what looked like a broken nose, an injured cheek bone (which turned out to be broken), and split upper and lower lips.

"The son of a bitch butted me, Mr. Hardy!"

I immediately grabbed him before he could lunge toward Kurt who instantly assumed a boxer's stance.

"You want some more of me? Come on. I got plenty more, Naylor!"

Since they both seemed ready and able I grabbed Kurt's arm so he could not commit and steered them down a hall through a mob of inquisitive kids, as some of them cheered one side or the other.

First, I escorted Kurt into Mrs. Jenkins' health suite, where she immediately confirmed my prognosis about the broken cheekbone. Then, I stepped out and told Mr. Naylor to get into Dr. Angel's office at once.

Now, just a minute; let's clear the air.

I'm Ryan Hardy, B.S., M.S, hired by Dr. Gordon Angel three days before the start of the current school year. The amazing thing was the only question he asked about my qualifications was how many education courses I had taken. And when I said none, he said "Welcome Aboard."

So far my two classes have been awesome! I've got kids who come in after school to work on their science fair projects. There is even another group I allow to hang out with me during lunch because they are so bright, I'm afraid of the consequences, if I don't. Actually, I love the vitality vibes surging about my head.

Kurt Naylor isn't one of the chosen few. This strange aura always surrounded him. Not that he isn't an excellent student. Just that he always seems to be on another plain … or drifting in an alien world when it comes to socializing. Oh, and he may be the only male who wore a long-sleeved dress shirt … all four seasons. I hear he's in a long sleeved sweat shirt in gym.

I hung around to see what was going down, but after ten or so minutes I was half-way out his waiting room when he opened the door and told me that all the kid would say was, "Call my Father. I can't tell you why I did it."

Dr. Angel declared he had just done that and needed an eye-witness. Naylor was sitting … actually his frame bent over, and his head and shoulders were resting in his lap. Angel told me his father was only five minutes away, and almost on key, Colonel Alex Naylor arrived, in uniform with four rows of various decorations.

From here on, the conversation between him and Angel is etched in my cerebral cortex forever. Angel explained the circumstances and his son's refusal to answer his questions why. Kurt's father nodded and when he had the chance turned to his son and asked, "What made you do this, Danny?"

Head still down he muttered, "He blocked me getting by him, called me a dirty Jew, and another Holocaust was coming. Then, he gave a Nazi salute and called me Juden frie! Father."

Colonel Naylor nodded and said that meant Jew Die! He told Kurt to show us why he became infuriated. It took almost a minute for the kid to get erect, unbutton his left sleeve, pull it back and turn his arm so it was palm up. At first I did not see the dark green numbers tattooed across his forearm, but Angel did.

I'll never forget the, "Oh Good God! He's a concentration camp survivor!"

Kurt slumped down again and silence reigned for over a minute. Until Angel suggested Kurt be sent to Mrs. Jenkins to get his bloodied face cleaned. He then had one of the office staff escort him after his Father agreed.

Colonel Naylor asked if The Boss wanted the full story and gave it when Angel said he had to have it all, and as detailed as possible. Then, Angel also added that he also wanted an eye witness, so I stayed.

"I was lost in a Jeep on some back German road April fourteenth, forty-five, the day after they gave up. I was desperately looking for any sort of help when a British unit rolled up and their Major told me to follow them. That as soon as they got to Bergan-Belsen he'd get in touch with my group. I had no idea what that was. About two hours later I wished I had stayed lost.

"Suddenly, it seemed like some alien force had lifted a curtain of stench so vile I had to use one hand to hold my nose, until I decided that wasn't doing any good. For maybe a full mile it grew until it seemed to be dripping off the sides of the Jeep. It was so bad I thought perhaps an errant shell had hit a Nazi poison gas dump. They did have lots of it. … So did we.

"Anyway, we rounded a sweeping bend and confronted twelve feet of barbed wire. Dr. Angel, there were emaciated bodies, some stark naked, strung along it, so perfectly spaced, it was obvious they had been hung by… I can't go on about that.

"When we reached it, there were hundreds of men and women clustered about the gate. Most just wore a single-pieced, gray, striped garment to cover their various states of starvation. I followed our guys. Corpses lay in scattered heaps … Piled up like they were ready for a trash collector.

"Our commander told me to go to work. Help anyone who looked like they could be saved. Take as many men as I needed. And then he vomited right at my feet.

"Hours later we got around to searching the barracks. The odors were so bad, we had to wear double operating masks, so we could at least breathe. The bunks were five high, no more than a foot separating each layer. Corpses and almost corpses inhabited a few, but most were vacant.

"I was ready to quit. Then, I thought I heard a cry. Right then I thought it was a rat … maybe a kitten. I asked one of my aides and he said he had heard it, too. That it seemed to be coming from under the bottom bunk in the aisle next to me.

"I bent down, saw what looked like a three-sided box and found Kurt. When I picked him up, he felt like the soiled bit of cloth wrapped around his midriff was his entire body weight. There was nothing there but tiny bones. But his whimpering told me somehow he had been fed enough to keep him alive.

"Dr. Angel, I was never able to confirm any details. I never located anyone who could tell me who the mother was. We were only there for a short day-and-a half so I didn't have time to find someone well enough to interpret for me. Frankly, I was overwhelmed. I didn't speak German and all the freed prisoners were in unbelievable states of malnutrition ... well, I just concentrated on keeping Kurt alive.

"Once we had time to examine him, it seemed humanly impossible that he was at least nineteen months old. That made things much simpler. After I found a Nanny I carted him around Europe with me for the next eighteen months.

"I came home and married Gretchen, whom I met in The Netherlands and we raised him and our two daughters."

Up until then The Boss hadn't spoken. Colonel Naylor said he would pay for any medical expenses, just as an ambulance rolled up, on full siren alert. Seems Davis needed hospital post haste.

When she swiped at Kurt's tangled hair, it turned out that his son had fragments from two of Davis's teeth imbedded in his forehead. Mrs. Jenkins had removed them, but wanted him to see a doctor ... immediately.

Then, The Boss told the colonel not to fret. To take his son to a doctor, then home, and he would be in touch some time tomorrow. And he told me to continue as his eye witness, so be ready to come when he called. He called at exactly 9:17 A.M.

Colonel, Mrs. Naylor and Kurt also Joel Davis's father and mother were waiting for me. Joel's face was swathed in a full bandage. They had already hired a lawyer and were ready to sue.

We all sat and The Boss began by asking Joel's parents if they knew what the Holocaust was? They said it was about killing people in the last war. But they didn't know any of the details.

Five minutes later they had some of the details. Both of them flinched whenever The Boss gave some of the methods. He detailed how people were shot while standing in mass graves they had dug. Or they were also jammed into trucks with a hose from the tail pipe spewing carbon monoxide killing all aboard … the gas showers and ovens cremating about four thousand innocents a day.

When they both almost begged him to stop, he gave them the low down on what their son had done … from the salute to the Juden frie, meaning Jews Die. Mrs. Davis sobbed as she silently stared at Joel, but his father yelled, "Where did you get the idea to do crap like this?"

Dr. Angel intervened. He told the Davis's they should make every effort to erase their son's beliefs. He also added that Joel was suspended for the rest of the school year. But he would be allowed to do course work and take finals.

That was twenty-nine years ago. I am retiring this June. Angel died the summer of ninety-nine. I was in Germany … yeah, seeing some of the Death Camps and I didn't know about his death till I got home. No cell phones back then. Just eleven years … some of our world has changed. The really nasty parts haven't. Have they?

The Ninth Moment: Grading Isn't Always Easy

Hi, I am Laura Dustin, and was Dr. Angel's Vice Principal, which is like saying I am a shadow fleeting through hallways never leaving a trace or echo. Well, maybe that is a little farfetched, but I have to be as honest as possible. Gordon is a legend. We can deal with that later. Let's just say that when he offered me this spot, I took it not because most future principals went though this; it was because I had to find out if all the rumors were really true.

So, it is the last three days when teachers are turning in grades, dismantling their rooms, and four first year teachers are filling out grade sheets in the Guidance Office. Later, Mrs. Lucas, told me Gordon had told them to do their work there.

Just before Lucille Nance, seventh grade Social Studies teacher closed her grading ledger *The Boss* walked in and dropped in a seat across from the quartet. After he asked how their year had gone, he reached over and took Nance's folder and spent a full minute or so reviewing it.

"Miss Nance, I've got a serious problem with your evaluation with four of your kids. Why are you giving them a D for the year when each of them got a C the first quarter, then three E's and a D for the year?"

"The county says if a student receives a C or better for any quarter grade they will pass for the year, Dr. Angel."

"Really? "His sandy thick eyebrows were escalated. "Have any of you others given grades like Miss Nance?"

Two nodded, and Gordon reached for each one's and checked.

"So, Mrs. Fisher, you passed three, and Miss Parley, you passed two. Can the three of you justify this before we go any further?"

"Dr. Angel, Billy Towers and Nick Little had me spending half my time demanding they behave. I can't tolerate getting them again in the fall."
The others voiced the same complaint, and reiterated the County's Grading Policy as a defense.

"How did they manage to get a passing grade one quarter? Did they suddenly reverse course? Or did you do that deliberately?"

When informed they would fail all of them, they refused. He amended the grades and advised them to apply for transfers. The next Fall none of them were on our roster. That has stayed with me for the twenty-one years I have been a principal.

The Tenth Moment:
Sometimes Bomb Shelters Do Not Shelter

It's Wednesday, the day after President Kennedy announced there was a Cuban Missile Crisis and we were placing a blockade to prevent The U.S.S.R. from sending intermediate- range- ballistic missiles to Cuba. That if we allowed this, the Soviet missiles were only ninety-minutes away from detonating extensive casualties on parts of our nation.

Dr. Angel called a faculty meeting as we were entering the building. This is about what he found out which caused him to call it. Well, maybe he was going to anyway. It was rumored the government was going to declare a national emergency any moment. We were really stressed. I even heard two or three teachers insisting that their classes be assigned to the boiler room, since it was below ground.

Let's break here and let me explain three vital points:

1. Ben Harrison Senior High was one story. It had a concrete base which allowed steel poles to be mounted every twelve feet. The rest of the outer structure was self-contained, pre-fabricated steel walls containing enclosed windows to be screwed into place. Today, three guys with electric screwdrivers could dismantle the entire building in less than two working days.

2. The Defense Department had published the effects that an H-Bomb of twenty mega- tons detonated within a mile of the Capitol would create. Everyone in a radius of six miles would be totally incinerated. The blast would follow at the rate of two thousand MPH for well over a mile beyond the flash point then decrease at the rate of about three-hundred miles per mile. Harrison was seventeen miles from the impact site. That meant it would be completely destroyed by the explosion's aftermath.

3. The boiler room was exactly four-feet deeper than Ben's terrazzo tiled floor ... get my point?

I'm not sure if any of my fellow doomed faculty knew about the first two, but I decided long before the crisis that I was going to have some fun. I told my classes that it was better to be boiled in midair than fried on the ground. So, I was selling a limited number of tickets for fifty-cents, to view the explosion from the top of the nearby water tower. And that Mr. Ford, a good friend of mine, would be throwing hamburgers up so we had a nice Last Supper. At first we were hurled into space by the force of the explosion, and then fried when the fire wall hit us full on.

When two of the Terrible Threesome, Fredrick, Wilson and Harper got wind of it, they rushed Dr. Angel's office. As usual neither of them saw the irony … well, except The Boss. He sent me a note saying he would like a ticket … immediately.

That was, of course a joke. I wasn't really selling tickets. Well, not for the Terrible Trio.

Now, about the meeting: Dr. Angel kept us waiting. Usually, he was waiting for us. When h did, he walked to stage center, slammed a packet on the podium and almost snarled, "I have just been informed that nineteen of you believe you have the right to go home if a national emergency is declared. May I be the first to tell that group and those who have not decided, your first and only obligation is to your students and their welfare."

That caused mummers, turning in seats and half-whispers, easily deciphered as angry frustration. However, nodding heads were an overwhelming majority.

"And for any of you who still believe you can desert your duties, I have procured enough school buses that if the occasion becomes desperate, I will have them placed at the parking lot entrances. Also I will have your cars monitored by male teachers."

Then, he told us to get back to our classrooms and see if we could help assuage our students' fears and anxieties.

It turned out none of this was needed, and the crisis was over. That was about two hours later when Kennedy announced the Russian flotilla carrying additional weapons had turned back and he hoped to schedule a meeting with the Soviets in the near future.

Songs for My Dwarf

And when I sue God for myself, he will see
within my eyes the tears of two.
~William Shakespeare

My Revelations

Once in a ...
(Time really stands still here)
God, or Whomever, blinks
And the exceptional
Those who bring changes
Which reshape our world
Slip through His nets ...
There are those who claim,
These are Unicorns!
I claim
You are one of the mistakes,
And only great mistakes
Cause catastrophic reforms
And revolutions.
You are one of these!

Birthings

It is our birthdays.
Mine was the years
Spent finding my art again
Yours was discovery
Of yourself!
Of your life's path,
Of your goals.

Absolutely

My mind, ideals and soul
Are joined to your generosity
Which constantly mocks
My frugalness.
To your selflessness
Quietly drowns my vanity
Only half in jest
I attempt this defense.
It is difficult
Being married to a Saint!
Just because of this
I am compelled to protect you
From those who would
Eagerly steal
Your energetic Halo.

What You Give Me

Because of your gifts,
I am allowed
To live in your special world.
Because of your love,
I dwell among waves of warmth.
Because of your grit,
I am forever amazed, enthralled,
And saved!

The Disillusioned Director

My writing creates
Worlds and galaxies
Six inches wide,
But yours creates
Their continents
And directs their river's flow!
I assemble characters
In sentences and paragraphs,
But you direct their Karmas
Rewarding periods or deletes!
I produce virtual movies
From pages spilling print,
But you are the director
Who polishes the scenes and actors!
And I would never have it be less
And I would never have it be any other way!

My Dwarf Goddess

There are
Times, glimpses, instants ...
(Yet none of these adverbs of time
Fit institution)
So, on occasions
Jammed between your hand
Your words and images,
I perceive ... No
My poet's eye,
My novelist ear
Captures ... No intrudes
On your rare, unselfish genes.
And not a bit awed,
I step aside and turn my camera eye
And recording ear to close-ups of you
Pushing a thousand idiots
Into the blessed chamber labeled
"Accomplished!"

Her Destiny

Wind chimes' tinkle
Accompany your flights ...
But not flights into the sky,
Journeys into the minds
Of those who need
Broken connections repaired.
Between the dreads and hopes
And on special occasions
You take me along
And that is when my life
Begins anew with you!

Safe Within My Dwarf's Crystal Ball

The maimed, wounded, bleeding and terrified
Dragging their failures
Arrive at my Dwarf's door
And somehow, she gives almost all
A life of less pain ...
A plan to run again ...
A star ...
Not just to guide
But one for their very own!
For ages, while slowly filling pages
And suffering lulls between edited rages
Has slowly brought me enlightenment...
And some when, through absent entitlement
I have come to accept the fact
She is not a Saint!
Even though she feels and annualizes,
Heals with voice and a hand
While her other one often leaves me breathless
It also cures me of dreaming my dreams...
Through hers!

Future Flowers

I sit among the bloomless children,
Who are starving for more than sun and water,
Seeking more than facts, dates and numbers
And I question, analyze...
Trying to make her realize her abilities
Expose her genius, as well as liabilities
Woman of my making,
But now beyond my imagination
Soar and meet your equals!
Touch the edges of eternity
Revive dead stars!
For you alone
Can erase unhealed scars!

Morning Songs

She ages before my eyes
Yet...magically does not grow old!
The new, isolated, long, gray strands
Form sprays of life
Which sparkle upon our pillows
Scenting them with our past
Her body has at last made peace
With both gravity and erosion
I have a vision of my Dwarf smiling
As she stands
Among ten thousand needy children

And

As she weaves and threads their lives
Into acceptable realities
She slowly becomes every blossom,
Every single sunrise,
Every evening drink,
And I think,
Just before I close my eyes,
That I see all of this
Gradually expanding among
These sparkling, gray strands

Reluctant Admissions

I have ceased to claim
She is orchards filled with apples
Or drooping cherry trees
Or wine in early autumn
To declare, That's what she means to me!
But
After two delicious decades
Of bazaars and native dress
I have a new outlook
A way to say this best...
Once you love a dwarf
Every site is new
Every day is Sunday
And every month is April!

Where is the Magic?

I have tried this so many times
In so many foreign lands
In one night camps
Or luxurious game parks...
I have taken pen
Seeking once again to tell you
How much beyond love
My feelings for you venture.

So, while Schuman's Traumerei
Whispers to me
Failed again...
My pen never runs out of ink
So, I think...
"I'll try again.
Next time...
Who knows?

More Dwarf Moments

I have never loved anyone
The way I love you
So mundane! But...
I hate how that allows you
Carte Blanche...totally!
So all I can do
Is wonder why I love you so ...
My reasoning defies words.

But you have always
Asked that I reach out . . .
Not up or not at all.
So, well,
I guess if this is not Eden.
You could really be my universe!

Ode to My Dwarf

I fell into your eyes,
Crawled into your thoughts,
Danced to your talents,
Strutted to your genius,
Longed for Compassion,
Hoped for your love,

And Won!

I am so. . . nothing. . .
No words describe
Yet. . .
There was nothing
But questions
Before you!
Now. . .
Only constant joy
And Pride!

Her Answer for Now . . . Perhaps Longer

Here's to my Tactile,
Favorite, Handsome,
Sweet, Warm, Tender
Competent, Clever, Intelligent,
Sexy, Huggable, Talented,
Thoughtful, Generous, Cuddly,
Gentle, Sensitive, Gifted,
Wonderful, Prizewinning, Strong,
Heat producing, Snuggly, Fuzzy,
Normal sized, Tried and True, Loyal,
Kissable, Hungry, Curious,
Good-looking,
Self-Sacrificing,
Tolerant,
Favorite Bear,
Who best of all,
Is Mine!

The Teacher's Mind Travels ... Also

Number I: Nothing But the Truth

Memories amass,
Then rush to
Newer, more
Lasting memory!

Somehow touching
Your mind
Now means more than kisses.

And therefore,
Lost among
Your thoughts I turn
To Paris,
As my Ally

Number II: Because ... I Have Chosen

I am forever the teacher, trapped but free
Because I take down stars and destroy dead seas.
Because my right hand points where the left cannot stay.
Because I recite words which recant a generations' dreams
And can summarize an eon with a phrase,
Because becomes more,
Because it covers all tenses.

Because I see gods die before they shave.
Because I hold no lamps, but often light false ways
Because I have honored dead things and manners
These dead things become banners
And only the past can live
After all my becauses ... will forever be ...
Because.

Number III: Class Instructions

Never weep for hurt and angry teachers
Each has carefully created their images.
Ignore the titles educator or professor
Most are disguised preachers
Shun those who advocate intolerance for all
Oh yes … read lots of Saint Paul.
And do not champion democracy
Its horizons have become too small.
Just open the door
Welcome them,
Let them in to you
As well as the classroom
Hug each one if you can
But always remember
You are only immortal
As long as you do not take
Anything more than
Their admiration

Number IV: The First Commandment

Historical observations occur
When God has blinded man again!

Light is only visible when blocked by matter.
It takes a great deal of talent to flee from one's genius.
Often a nervous breakdown is required for one's sanity.
We run from our greatest fears until they capture us.
Education is obtained despite attending school.
Problems diminish as fat increases.
Stones and gods fall at the same rate of speed.
When stripped, one is no longer naked.

Who does not destroy what they love the most?
The tortured will always worship their tormentor.
Conclusion ...
Obsessions, paradoxes and observations
Are never permanent,
Because they are never pertinent!

Number V: Am I Teacher or Ringmaster?

Every age has a Pied Piper
Able to create
Enough magic which
Allowing his listeners
To single out one star
From all the heavens,
One leaf from
The entire forest
And make them their own.
Because the Piper
Is the master of mediocrity
Everyone laughs or hums along,
As they clap their hands in time to
Pseudo magic dreams the Piper plays.

Number VI: Am I Teacher or Sorcerer

By making magic the teacher
Blots out changes the world goes through
If their magic is great, a dome is erected
Which life or death cannot penetrate
Each sorcerer brings their own illusions,
Reality changes with every act.
In between, clowns make students
Grin at mirrors less intricate ... more clear
If there are no artifacts, there is no magic
Magic leaves only mystery
Only clowns sanctify our amusements
And solidify our faiths
Because ...
The Sorcerer needs the audience.
The audience needs the magic.
And the magic needs applause.

Number VII: The Babe's Mouth Holds Fangs

The tutor of geniuses asked
His six year old charge,
"So, where do you
Think God lives?"
"Doctor Hines," he replied,
"God lives alone …
Beyond the stars
Where all is blackness
In a house
He cannot leave
Because we won't let him."
And as the tutor paused
Wondering where and when
All his intelligence disappeared to
The six year old sighed and took
Another slurp
Of his cheery ice cream cone

Number VIII: Lost Among the Apps

I watch adolescents of all ages
Come and go
Ignoring more than Michelangelo…
Eyes glued to ill-shaped phones
Reducing life, love or death
To less than my hand size.

And as their worlds expand
Its dimensions do not,
Yet, no one dares to yell
Beware! Take care!
God's not the only demon
In there!

Number IX: My Rejected Request

It's time to come!
Just for the brief,
Less than three-billionths
Of your life span,
Time to embrace
The wonders you
Refuse to admit
Are poised just beyond
The confines of the box
Your prejudices have
Forced you to erect
It doesn't present fear or terror
Just Change!

Number X: A Teacher's Silent Declaration

All the names were changed
To protect the guilty
 And the personas exaggerated
To make a Point!
Time and place are irrelevant
The teacher's world would screw them up!

These timeless, placeless tales
Have occurred since the first kid
Went to school
So, you can't sue!

The stories are not about your dumbness
They are about dumb-asses
Who assume reading and writing
The only criteria
Intelligence and/or intellect
And believe it or not
This is the majority!

Number XI: The Teacher's Wish List

Trying to reach a world
With only one time zone,
Where things are mostly right or wrong
Where those who are right are good,
And those who are wrong are bad,
I ask for the world between my teeth
So I can bite until it screams!
Forgive me for being absurd,
Forgive me for spending so long
Searching for the place where my time will mesh.
Where I no longer need to explain
Why my watch always had other faces
And without hands
And has never told time in an ordinary sense
Yet - remembers every second it and I have been exiled.
So I wish to reach out my hands
Hold my breath while waiting for fulfillments...
Or my hands to fall off into a better time

Number XII: The Historian

When I was a kid
The restless ones fled.
Some joined the French Foreign Legion
Others slipped away to fight in Spain.
A few became bums
And saw the nation
From fast moving freight cars.
A few went into the boxing ring,
The desperate jumped out of office windows.
But for those few
Who, on yeasty August nights,
Heard the caravan's camel bells
Passing beneath their windows
And chased their dreams,
Which for the few
Did come true ...
I can not
Find their records.

Number XIII: The Demented Four Horsemen

Harold could quote Kant, Spinoza and Guide
For hours on end
And died ...
Richard marked off the days
From *Sin*-day nights to *Fry*-day afternoons
Cursing the bastards who never worked a day
And died ...
Herman spent forty years leaning over the sides of ships
Wondering what the porpoises said,
Remembered Francis of Assisi's words at night
And died ...
Chester, Harold's twin brother, was a mute
Never took a single step,
Laid still like a dead stick,
Staring into the nursery ceiling,
Until he was forty-five
When he stopped breathing...
Did he die?

Number XIV: Shouting From My Mirror

As a teacher I proclaim
History is a series
Of ladies sitting
Before the same vanity, totally out of sync
With their backgrounds
Even the frame!
But never the subject …
So sit lady sit.
And as time ebbs
And recedes about your feet,
Do not question the validity or purpose.
Never despise your reflections.
Only pay attention
Some say history takes its time
That only major events bridge the ages
Like a conjunction until both flow
Like a body not like droplets.
To the play and its actors
This new era
I say, *"No."*

Number XV: Not One Single Regret

All my words are gone … stolen … sons and daughters took a
few
But all the others went to those I hardly knew.
Ragamuffins, student gangsters … one generation of middle
class fools
And of course a priest or two joined my Apathetic Apostles
Who prospered on the threads of what they thought they
knew.

I gave pearls away for instant applause …
for belly laughs from fools and frogs.
Ten thousand volumes of reflections thrown into that pool that
is youth...
Gave all of it without right or wrong … now more or less its
gone!
Sunken into wall to wall carpets or drying in sanitary
bedrooms,
Or buried in preformed concrete tombs, along Potomac shores,
And if all of it began again, this time I would play the clam
Or run deep into the trees to save my thoughts
For a way-ward squirrel or doe
No I would not!
If somehow I still care … if I still remember names and
wonders
It is because, Bez,
 I cannot spit out the stardust I saw
In yours, and a few other dozen or so eyes.

Number XVI: My Revelations

Once in a ...
(Time really stands still here)
God, or whomever blinks
And *The Exceptional,*
Those who bring changes
Which reshape our world ...
Slip through His nets ...

There are those who claim
These are Unicorns!
I claim
Perhaps you are one of those mistakes
And only great mistakes
Cause catastrophic reforms
And revolutions

XVII: The Many Mirrors' Letters

Less than sixty days from today
I will be asked to give up living …
Then be asked to teach about life.
I will be asked to surrender my freedom …
Then be an instructor on democracy
I will be asked to ignore social injustices …
Then be considered an expert on social sciences,
Entrusted to train tomorrow,
Endow it with strict objectivity.
But I say:
Less than sixty days from now
I shall continue to amaze
I shall continue to amuse
The multi personalities
I introduce each day as me!

Number XVIII: What Were Their Names?

I remember a hundred Marians
Yet, both male and female faces
Swimming through crowded spaces

I remember
Some were smart even pretty
Others not so fortunate

Yet, all become portraits
And I remember and remember
What was not important

How they chose their friends
What was most sensitive

The cruelty their youth
At times, parents created
Trying to make amends
I remember!

But not in proper order
After some gentle time thief
Suddenly stole their teacher's pen.

Number XIX: A Belated Confession

Before the last class ends
As parts of my past
No longer seem to last
Long enough to become a memory
As my history is fixed
And I surrender
To Nature's wisdoms
Let me feast one last time
Amidst my students'
Multi talented glow

For they and they alone
Were able to claim my heart
But not destroy me.

Number XX: My Last Lament

It just isn't right!
I aged at the speed of light
Because all my students stole
More than they deserved
So, at ninety or so
I still have a full head of hair
Totally gray and each strand bears
A plundering student's name
Clamoring to proclaim
They are my Crown of Thorns.

XXI: The Director

Above all else
In spite of myself
Ghost's forces
Give me just one role
When the anxious ones
Sob and cry.
"Am I crazy?
Can I do this?
Is this wrong?
Will I be ridiculed?"

I have always known
That I was there
Only to answer, *"No!"*
Because ghost's forces always
Told me this is my role ...
That my *No,* must be so.
So, but not true. So,
But not right. So,
But not forever
And my *No* is so
Just long enough so
All the wonderful Crazies
Have a model ...
Not a solution.

XXII: Etude for Bez

Doors for you
Are hopes or outlets
So, when you place your ear
Silence has noise!
But not chaotic
Voices debating
Those eternal questions ...
Who am I?
Where am I?
What is my relationship
To my fellow man?
And to the universe?

And you believe
There are many doors
And many debtors.

To which I say,
You are among
These very few.

Epilogue

The most difficult thing to read is time.
Maybe because it changes so many things.
~Erin Morgenstern

The Students' Gifts

Because you bestow so many gifts
I am allowed to live
In all your special worlds.

Because of these
I dwell among waves of warmth.

Because of your grit and determination
I am forever amazed, enthralled,
Even saved from assuming
I too may be- *a god!*